Necromancer Troubles

LIANA BROOKS

OTHER WORKS

ALL I WANT FOR CHRISTMAS

All I Want For Christmas Is A Reaper
All I Want For Christmas Is A Werewolf

FLEET OF MALIK

Bodies In Motion
Change of Momentum

HEROES AND VILLAINS

Even Villains Fall In Love
Even Villains Go To The Movies
Even Villains Have Interns
Even Villains Play The Hero (books 1 – 3 omnibus)
The Polar Terror

TIME AND SHADOWS

The Day Before
Convergence Point
Decoherence

SHORTER WORKS

Fey Lights
Prime Sensations
Darkness and Good

Find other works by the author at
www.lianabrooks.com

Necromancer Troubles

INKLET #100

LIANA BROOKS

Inkprint PRESS

www.inkprintpress.com

Print ISBN: 978-1-922434-33-3
eBook ISBN: 9798201903909

www.inkprintpress.com

National Library of Australia Cataloguing-in-Publication Data
Brooks, Liana 1982 –
Necromancer Troubles
44 p.
ISBN: 978-1-922434-33-3
Inkprint Press, Canberra, Australia
1. Fiction—Fantasy—Urban 2. Fiction—Fantasy—Contemporary 3. Fiction—Short Stories

First Print Edition: February 2023
Cover photo © Jonas Svidras via Pixabay
Cover design © Inkprint Press
Interior art © Amy Laurens

NECROMANCER TROUBLES

"Wʜᴀᴛ ᴅᴏ ʏᴏᴜ ʀᴇᴍᴇᴍʙᴇʀ?" I ᴀsᴋᴇᴅ the person across the metal table from me. There was no sound in the interrogation box except the ripple of the artificial stream running from the north wall across the table and filtering out on the south end, where the mirrored glass allowed the rest of my team to watch. There couldn't be any ticking clocks, tapping pens, or ominous chimes; one never knew what could trigger the magically touched.

The person across from me was six three, brown eyed, blond haired, age fifty-seven, and dead. In life Matt Ferison had lived a blameless life as an adjunct mathematics professor at the local college. He'd died of a cancer that went too long ignored and had been buried by grieving relatives who, while all being terribly upset at his loss, did not seem the kind of the people to illegally raise a man from his grave and leave him to wander around downtown Cherry Tree, Pennsylvania.

A few of them looked like the sort who could tap a ley line, but they would have taken him home and he would have been Not My Problem.

Instead I was spending Saturday night with a dead man wearing peeling layers of funeral makeup, a skewed toupee, and a shirt being held together in the back by safety pins because he was bloating as he decomposed.

Matt shook his head in the slow, zombie way the recently risen have. "Not much. I know my name. I—"

"Think about the necromancer," I said as gently as I could. "I know who you are. I need to know who they are. Did they give you a name?"

"My name is Matt," Matt repeated for something like the nine hundredth time in twenty minutes. "I have a name."

"Did the necromancer say what their name was?"

Another slow shake. "Not that I remember. Maybe they said it where I couldn't hear. But I didn't hear. So I don't know."

"Did the necromancer tell you to call them anything?"

This time Matt nodded, slowly pitching his whole torso forward and rocking back. "Yes."

"What did the necromancer tell you to call them?"

"God."

The pen very nearly snapped in my hand from frustration. "God?" I kept my tone light through gritted teeth. "Did they happen to mention *which* god? Did they mention a pantheon? Did you see anything that might have been a religious symbol? Was the necromancer wearing special clothes?"

"They wore jeans. And a shirt with symbols on it."

"Did you recognize any of the symbols."

"They looked like letters."

Another twenty torturous minutes passed and Matt had successfully told me the necromancer was wearing a *Dark Kitti* heavy metal band t-shirt and probably a pair of Nikes. I thanked him for his time and handed him over to the departure team, who would circumspectly contact his family, ask them if there were any lingering questions or if they needed to raise him from his grave. If they said no, he'd be returned to the cemetery and banished to whatever afterlife awaited him. If he was needed, he'd be suited up for a meeting with the family, allowed to talk with them, and *then* dropped in his grave and banished.

Either way, he had it better than I did. Matt was going to his eternal rest. All I had was twelve resurrected randos and zero leads.

"Could be worse," my friend Kelly said with sympathy as I exited the magic-killing rain and toweled off. "You could be dealing with a necromancer who wants to keep them alive. As it is, this looks like a prank."

"What I don't get," said Phil from the next desk over, "is who would go through all this effort."

I tossed my towel in a yellow bin marked Hazardous Wash and shrugged. "It's like a street artist who paints sublime landscapes on the side of trains. It's magical graffiti. Some people do it for the love of the activity, not the fame."

"There's no fame in being a necromancer," Kelly said.

"But there are lucrative contracts," I said. "And our necromancer friend doesn't seem to care. If it were me, I would definitely only bring back rich people and ask for their passwords. Do it in the morgue. Get the details before the family locks anything down. Banish them. Boom! Easy money."

Phil frowned at me. "That's a highly specific plan."

"Some people spent their teen years choreographing social media dances, I planned necromancy heists. Doesn't mean any of us did the things we planned."

I totally did, but only enough to fund college, buy a car, and put a little to the side so I could retire comfortably when I was old enough to retire.

The key to success was never taking enough for the family to notice and never bringing back someone whose family was likely to summon a necromancer of their own.

Unethical, definitely.

Lucrative, also definitely.

Looking at the list of files I needed to sort and the reports that needed to be written, I sighed. "I'm going home. This will keep until Monday."

"That's a good idea," Kelly said. "You look exhausted."

"It's been a long week in the ley lines." I grabbed my bag and waved to everyone. Three o'clock on a Saturday morning and I was stepping out of the precinct, not someone's bedroom, in the chill and somewhat damp spring morning.

The drive home was short, just a quick run down Main to Cherry Street, across the west branch of the Susquehanna River, and right on Front Street, left on Peach Alley. There was a little cluster of new apartments that had been built about the same time the new canals had been put in. Thirty tiny studios that offered an alternative to student housing. Most of the people who lived here were single, with a scattering of young families and couples.

I parked outside my building in one of the guest spots because my reserved spot was taken. Again. Slamming my car door shut, I looked at the second story apartment above mine. Yes, there were low lights on.

Grumbling to myself, I tried to remember what terrible leap of logic had led me to this life of general law-abiding goodness. Working for the department was a logical job for someone with magical skill, but that didn't mean I cared about justice. Honestly, I think I was in it for the health benefits. If this country ever gets affordable healthcare for all, I'm out.

For now, the cost of my seasonal allergy medicine was enough to keep me in a mind-numbing job that barely paid the rent.

The stairs creaked under my weight.

So let me change that thought...

For now, the cost of my seasonal allergy medicine was enough to keep me in a mind-numbing job that barely paid the rent on a termite-riddled apartment one hard sneeze from falling down. I either needed a nationwide healthcare plan or someone I knew to conveniently drop dead so I could have a plausible reason for the pile of cash I had sitting in an off-shore account.

"Hey!" I pounded on my upstairs neighbor's door, glaring down at the punk's little black four-door that was parked where my car belonged. "Hey! I know you're up!"

Four seconds later the door fell open to reveal a skinny grad student with a straggly beard and skin nearly gray from the sixteen computer monitors currently all showing a melee screen from *Legends of Feywar*.

I raised an eyebrow. "I guess your dissertation is going well."

"Eh..." He looked guiltily at the screens an academic grant had bought him last summer. "Study break?"

"Study break? Man..." I shook my head. "You've been living here for six years and you've been on a 'study break' for five of them. Get it together."

"I will, I will," he promised. "I'm just not sure where to go with my research right now. There's some promising leads and I—"

"You used that line your third year."

"As soon as the grant—"

I shook my head. "Last year."

My neighbor rolled his eyes. "What do you want? I have headphones on. I'm quiet as a ghost. Why are you banging on my door? You're killing me!" He pointed to the melee screen where his character was taking two HP damage for every hobgoblin stab.

Rolling my eyes, I reached out and smacked him upside the head.

"Ow! Police brutality!"

"I'm not the police."

"Ow! Fey Warden brutality!" He rubbed his head. "What was that for? Did someone drop iron in your twinkies?"

"The unlicensed necromancy?" I stared at him. "It needs to stop. If I have to file one more report about a lost or abandoned undead, I will personally put you in the morgue."

His face furrowed in furious frustration.

(Yes, I do love the alliteration. The laws of moral decency, ethics, and the land aren't the only ones I regularly break.)

"But, I was so careful! How did you know?"

"Because you turn your car headlights on when you load your gear and
your car headlights *point directly into my
bedroom* because you're *using my car
space!*" I pointed down at his offending
car. "Every night you've woken me up,
I find an unlicensed zombie case on my
desk the next morning. Why?"

He looked guiltily at the floor. "I
heard they were talking about budget
cuts at the department and I wanted to
make sure you kept your job."

I rolled my eyes skyward and stared
at the moldering ceiling of the breeze-
way. I didn't know whether to be
touched he'd thought of it, or insulted
that he didn't think I'd already have a
solution. "Couldn't you just write a
letter to the editor like everyone else?"

"I thought this was more effective.
You know, direct action."

"Great. Thanks. Apology accepted.
Do it again and I might not put you in
the morgue, but I *will* put you behind

burning bars of magic and leave you there. And, tomorrow?" I raised an eyebrow. "Get your car out of my parking space."

THE MAKING OF *NECROMANCER TROUBLES*

I wish I had some entertaining story that goes with this but I really don't. It's based entirely on my memories of living in some off-campus apartments in college and hearing about shenanigans (not actual corpse-raising though) that were perfectly timed with my noisy neighbor's comings and goings.

It was just partying and prank wars, nothing that escalated to needing the police, but when a daily writing challenge came up asking for a short story about an inconvenient necromancer this is what I came up with. May it bring you freedom from all annoying neighbors forever.

Read more by Liana Brooks!

ALL I WANT FOR CHRISTMAS IS A WEREWOLF

THERE WAS MISTLETOE OVER MY DESK. Honest to goodness mistletoe hanging over the remains of my Halloween festivities. The Great Pumpkin was now overshadowed by a hemiparasitic shrub.

When I'd left for a conference two hours ago, my desk had been a bastion against the winter holidays. A snow-free island in an otherwise elegantly decorated office suite dedicated to art.

The gallery's front foyer with the dark wood paneling and over-stuffed pine-green tub chairs was now displaying glass and metal snowflakes in dazzling designs.

The main negotiating room, with the long table suitable for a fleet of lawyers, had a festive Seasons Greetings banner with pine trees and bright red birds signed by various Miami athletes.

The hall had garlands, multi-colored lights, and occasionally holiday music blaring out of incautiously opened offices.

But this?

This monstrous greenery was not supposed to touch my space.

Elegant Miami's main art gallery across the MacArthur Causeway was a glittering gem of holiday art. But over here, at the offices on Miami Beach that had been selected specifically to be near my boss's favorite house, things were toned down.

This was where Elegant Miami hid the nitty gritty details of business. It was the safe space for the sales people that spent all day on the phone with overseas clients; it was the home base of the style teams who went and decorated Miami palaces with carefully curated art from around the world; it was a soulless sovereignty of the contracts office where Maureen and I made sure every jot and tittle were in place.

Tittle was one of my co-worker's favorite words. It means the dot over a lower case I or J, but it sounds funny. Stuck in an L-shaped, linoleum-floored concrete bunker with two high windows that looked at the neighboring building a foot away and that always smelled of nail polish and mildew, we took our fun where we could find it.

But I drew the line at plastic Naughty Santa window clings blocking the little sunlight available. Being held hostage by forced holiday cheer was not part of my paycheck.

"Happy holidays, Del!" Maureen jumped out from behind my desk wearing a bright blue sweater with silver bells, dancing elves, and snowflakes. The bell at the end of her bright pink

Santa hat with pole dancing elves jingled as she stilled.

I stared, carefully counting to ten in every language I could remember, willing the other half the contracts team to vanish. It wasn't enough. Maureen and her seasonal cheer remained where they were.

"Don't you love it? I'm going to spray some fake snow too!" She pointed around at the sad, red tinsel garlands hanging off the black filing cabinets and the tiny palm tree that was sagging under a strand of rainbow lights.

"That's really not necessary," I said carefully circling around the hazardous airspace of the parasitic plant of unwanted kisses.

What was Maureen even thinking? Who on earth was I going to kiss here? It was against my personal policy to kiss clients or married people. That left Rafael Kane, office grinch, as the only possible target of unwanted contact.

Granted, he was a hot and sexy Office Grinch, but he was also the person voted most likely to ruin a party. He didn't chitchat. He didn't get distracted. He didn't waste time talking to coworkers, going to long Friday lunches, or building friendships.

Rafael Kane went to work, smiled for his clients only, and made Elegant Miami over fifteen percent of our yearly profit. We all loved him for his sales acumen, and stunning good looks, but no one around here considered him a friend.

Very early on, I'd tried. But Rafael Kane had taken one look at me, snarled like I'd stabbed his grandma, and avoided me ever since.

Which suited me just fine.

I frowned. If Maureen thought there was any chance of an office romance, my desk would look like an ad for the Great Bridal Expo. I needed tiny white seed pearls and chiffon as much as I needed mistletoe, which was about as much as a shark needed a tuba.

My idea of a good date was streaming a good murder mystery. I liked crime shows, creepy horror movies, and all things Halloween. People joked that I was a pagan, but that wasn't exactly true. I just loved the idea of magic. It made sense to me.

I should have loved the idea of Santa, except I can't remember a time I wasn't poor, and Santa doesn't visit poor kids.

December was my own personal hell. No winter solstice bonfire would ever be big enough to burn away all my anger at the forced cheer, demand for gifts, and unseasonable expectations.

I wasn't making New Year's Resolutions, I did that on my birthday in July.

I wasn't meeting anyone under the mistletoe, I wasn't that desperate.

I wasn't going to participate in the annual gift exchange, because somehow I always wound up with the bar of soap stolen from the pay-by-the-hour motel down the street.

I would be skipping the party, hitting the white sand beaches of Miami with a pink drink in hand, and spending my three days off catching up on N.W. Gehson's *Serial Killerz* series.

Maureen moved out from behind my desk and pouted. All of five-foot-nothing, she was a cute, apple-shaped woman with sunset pink hair and perpetually purple lips from a permanent makeup choice she made thirty years ago when she was twenty-one, drunk, and planning to be an exotic dancer all her life.[1]

In the bright blue sweater, she

---

[1] She still dances under the name Cotton Candy every other Friday down at the Sugar Strip on 4th, if you're wondering.

looked like the world's glummest Sugar Plum Fairy. She was holding a shiny blue paper with the words "All I Want For The Holidays" and a blank space for a holiday wish on it.

If I ignored the paper, I might escape further holiday interrogations.

"I… I was just trying to be nice!" A huge tear shimmered in her eye.

"I know." I patted her shoulder and tried very hard not to look at the tattoo peeking above her collar that HR insisted she keep covered during work hours. "But I don't like Christmas."

"This year is going to be different!" Maureen assured, her smile turning on like a floodlight in turtle season. "I figured out why you don't like Christmas."

"Because it's a commercial farce to celebrate capitalism?"

"No, silly! Because you're single! No one's giving you the good gifts." She winked and tried to bump me with her hip, but since her head only comes up to my shoulder even in kitten heels, it didn't quite work.

I scooted around her and into my three-sided box of an office.

There were sparkly confetti snowflakes covering the nameplate that had been a gift from one of my favorite metal-work artists.

Delinna Farmer was not a name that deserved to have snow on it. Especially fake snow.

Shaking the snow off the metal cut-out of my name, I smiled up at Maureen. "Really, Maureen, I'm fine."

"You will be!" She pulled a scroll of candy pink paper out of her cleavage so it unrolled in a long, curling list. "This is Auntie Maureen's list of acceptable bachelors in the greater Miami area."

"Maureen," I said, sitting down and giving her my very best glare, "if Rafael Kane is mentioned even once on that list, I will murder you. Right here and now. There will be blood all over your dancing elf sweater. No jury will convict me."

She rolled her eyes. "Tried that. Obviously there's chemistry there, but Rafe could have chemistry with a doorknob, so it doesn't matter." She put the list of names—written in pink and purple ink—on my desk. "Names. Numbers. Histories. Sizes."

"Siz—Oh!" I covered my mouth. "Sweet mother of pearl! Maureen! This is so invasive!" I crumpled the list up and dropped it in the recycling bin.

"A girl's got to know…"

"I do not need to know anyone's sizes!" I shouted as the door to the contracts office opened and the devil himself walked in.

Rafael's brown eyes went wide, his tan face frozen in a rictus of horror.

"I'm not participating in the company Christmas party and I'm not ordering the shirts," I said loudly, willing

Maureen to play along. Rafael might be the office grinch, but nobody gossiped as much as his people in the sales department. If he even guessed at the content of Maureen's list, I'd have every art gallery employee and intern in the greater Miami area sending me extra details.

Maureen, oblivious to the threat of Dick Pic Armageddon, crossed her arms over her ample chest. "Why not? What's wrong with the holiday party?"

"Because..." I scrambled for an excuse that wouldn't insult Maureen's party planning. "...I'm seeing someone."

Rafael snorted in amusement as he shook his head and walked to our copy machine by the door. The sales department had a better one, one that could print posters and banners, but it was broken and the sales associates had been bouncing in and out of the contracts office all week. There was nothing like the holidays to convince the obscenely wealthy to drop hundreds of thousands of dollars on art.

"Oh, sweetie," Maureen said, grabbing my arm and leaning in for a sideways hug as she ignored Rafael. "You don't need to lie."

"I'm not," I lied. "I am in a relationship. And I think it's serious. We are talking about moving in together."

From the copier Rafael gave me a look of disbelief that said, *No one would ever live with you.*

Maureen patted my hand with a tiny sigh of pity. "Let me guess. His name is Nick 'The Closer' Claus and you ordered him from the toys department at Lady Things downtown? I've met him too." Her smile was wicked. "But he doesn't count as a dinner date."

Too. Much. Information.

Closing my eyes, I focused on the filing list I needed to finish today. Anything to get the image of my middle-aged co-worker gleefully bouncing through the adult toy store out of my head.

In my imagination, she wore a frilled pink skirt that barely covered her ample thighs. I shuddered.

My only option was to lie more, or to hope Rafael would step in to help me. "Maureen—"

"No!" Rafael shouted from across the room. "No more. Not until I leave. I do not need to hear this. Let me finish. Please. Five more pages!"

Just for that I wanted to play dirty, but encouraging Maureen would give me a heart attack. There was only one course of action left...

"I'm getting a dog," I said before the dick pics became porno subscriptions in my stocking. "I've been visiting the shelters and I'm planning to adopt one over the holidays."

Maureen's shoulders sagged. "Honey, that does not count."

"A dog will be more loyal than any man will!" I drew myself up, a furious dark queen with a mask of rage perfected after years of studying every campy Halloween vampire movie ever. Morticia Addams, eat your heart out. "Probably more loyal than a woman, too. It'll love me, wait for me, and cuddle with me while I watch horror movies in December. A dog won't make me watch cheesy Christmas specials. A dog will go for walks on the beach with me. A dog will be happy eating whatever I cook—"

"A dog should have a high-protein diet."

Maureen and I both turned to stare.

Had Rafael Kane actually joined a conversation that wasn't about sales? After all these years?

"Do you like dogs?" Maureen asked politely, reverting back to Sweet Office Eccentric like a chameleon. "You've never mentioned them."

Rafael stared at the wall behind the copier as he realized his mistake. His body went rigid and I swear I saw a shiver of terror shimmy through him. He knew Maureen would never let him escape now.

"My mother raised dogs when I was growing up." He finished his copy work and turned to glare at me. "I've seen the stuff you eat for lunch, Del. Do the world a favor and stick to stuffed animals and battery-operated toys. A dog deserves better." He opened his mouth as if he were going to continue, then snapped it shut and marched out, back stiff.

Maureen hummed happily. "He has such a nice tush!"

"Maureen!" I smacked her arm.

"What? I'm married, not dead."

"We're at work."

"Quitting time was eight minutes ago. I can lust after people off the clock."

"You are a dirty old woman."

"Yes I am," she said proudly.

I rolled my eyes and remembered why I'd come back in. "I need to get my water bottles. I keep forgetting them." Nine of them sat in a row by my spare shoes.

"Oh, is that what happened?" Maureen asked. "I thought you'd decided to decorate with them. Maybe make a shrine to your beloved *agua*."

"Ha ha, funny." I grabbed a big bag with the name of a local farmer's stall on it and stuffed the water bottles inside. "The winter wonderland stuff. Can you keep it off my desk?"

Maureen pouted again.

"Please? I'll bring you some of those spiced pecans you like." If the bodega had a BOGO sale going on. If it wasn't buy-one-get-one, I wasn't sharing.

Her eyes went wide with delight. "Consider it gone. I will leave your corner a natural wasteland of bones, ghouls, and whatever that thing is," she said pointing to my Zany Zombie bobblehead.

"Thank you." I packed up and went home to research animal shelters. If I was going to be forced to participate in the holidays, I deserved to have someone who was happy to see me every day.

Surely I could get a dog for Christmas. It couldn't be that hard.

Keep reading! Head to
www.inkprintpress.com/liana
brooks/christmas/werewolf/
to buy your copy now!

ABOUT THE AUTHOR

While LIANA BROOKS has never lived next door to a necromancer, she's not adverse to the idea—so long as they're quiet. In said quiet, Liana enjoys writing science fiction in every form, from sprawling space operas romances (the *Fleet of Malik* series) to the antics of a super-powered family (the *Heroes and Villains* series).

Liana also maintains a soft spot for paranormal romances. She writes the popular *All I Want For Christmas* novellas, including *All I Want For Christmas Is A Werewolf* and *All I Want For Christmas Is A Reaper*.

You can learn more about her and her books at www.LianaBrooks.com.

INKLET #083
Dancer, Dreamer Seer
LIANA BROOKS

INKLET #084
As Time Whirls Slowly Past
AMY LAURENS

INKLET #085
Far More Satisfying Than Hell
AMY LAURENS

INKLET #086
Just Another Day In Hell
LIANA BROOKS

INKLET #087
Moon AND Morning
AMY LAURENS

INKLET #088
Some Impropriety Expected
AMY LAURENS

INKLET #089
NEON SNOW
LIANA BROOKS

Reincarnation
LIANA BROOKS

INKLET #091
More Than Mushrooms
AMY LAURENS

DOUBLE ISSUE
How To Make A Star
& The World Ended
LIANA BROOKS

CAUGHT
IN THE ACT
AMY LAURENS

ANUBIS
Has Sent You
Six Souls
LIANA BROOKS

PRAYER TO A
GODDESS
LIANA BROOKS

Love In The
Time Of Corona
AMY LAURENS

RECRUITMENT
AMY LAURENS

IDENTITY
Theft 101
LIANA BROOKS

Curses
With Benefits
AMY LAURENS

NECROMANCER
TROUBLES
LIANA BROOKS